READ TO ME, GRANDMA

PUBLICATIONS INTERNATIONAL, LTD.

Cover illustrated by Richard Bernal
"Read to Me, Grandma" illustrated by Jan Foletta

Louis Weber, C.E.O.
Publications International, Ltd.
7373 North Cicero Avenue
Lincolnwood, Illinois 60712

Ground Floor, 59 Gloucester Place
London W1U 8JJ

www.pilbooks.com

Manufactured in China.

8 7 6 5 4 3 2 1

ISBN 1-4127-0459-6

Read to Me, Grandma

When you ask me to read to you,
　　With your gentle voice so sweet,
I look into your bright, wide eyes
　　And quickly take a seat.
For in this world, I promise,
　　There is nothing I'd rather do
Than sit and share this storybook
　　With a child as sweet as you.
Of course I'll read to you, my dear,
　　It fills my heart with pride
That I could be the lucky one
　　To read right by your side.

TABLE OF CONTENTS

The Owl & the Pussycat

Written by Edward Lear Illustrated by Carolyn Croll

The Owl and the Pussycat went to sea
   In a beautiful pea-green boat:
They took some honey,
   And plenty of money
Wrapped up in a five-pound note.

The Owl looked up to the stars above,
   And sang to a small guitar,
"O lovely Pussy, O Pussy, my love,
   What a beautiful Pussy you are,
You are, you are!
   What a beautiful Pussy you are!"

Pussy said to the Owl, "You elegant fowl,
    How charmingly sweet you sing!
Oh! let us be married; too long we have tarried:
    But what shall we do for a ring?"
They sailed away, for a year and a day,
    To the land where the bong-tree grows;
And there in a wood a Piggy-wig stood,
    With a ring at the end of his nose,
His nose, his nose,
    With a ring at the end of his nose.

        "Dear Pig, are you willing to sell for one shilling
            Your ring?" Said the Piggy, "I will."
        So they took it away, and were married next day
            By the Turkey who lives on the hill.
        They dined on mince and slices of quince,
            Which they ate with a runcible spoon;
        And hand in hand, on the edge of the sand,
            They danced by the light of the moon,
        The moon, the moon,
            They danced by the light of the moon.

Grandma's Scrapbook

Written by Kate Hannigan   Illustrated by Jan Foletta

It was Hopper's day to visit his Grandma, and he had some big plans. "Let's hop right down to the pond, Grandma," he said as he burst through the front door.

When Hopper got excited, he just couldn't slow down.

He bounced all around Grandma's living room, rattling the teacups and bumping into the furniture.

"We can go swimming, and we can have a picnic, and we can play chase!" Hopper said without stopping to take a breath.

Hopper loved going to Grandma's house, and he always looked forward to their special adventures together.

Grandma was happy to see Hopper. She loved her grandson, and she especially liked the fun they had together.

"You're more bouncy than a bucketful of frogs!" laughed Grandma when she saw Hopper.

Hopper smiled a huge smile.

Grandma thought Hopper acted just like she did when she was a little bunny—always excited and eager for a new and exciting adventure.

Just as the bunnies sat down to make their plans for the day, there was a loud *boom!* Thunder shook their house, and little Hopper scurried to the window to look outside.

"It's raining," he cried. "Now the day is ruined!"

Grandma told him not to worry. And quick as lightning, she came up with another plan.

"I'm really sorry, little bunny," Grandma said. "We may not be able to get to the pond, but I think I have something you might enjoy."

Hopping over to the bookshelf, Grandma pulled down a big scrapbook. They opened the cover, and Hopper pointed at the pictures.

"Grandma, that bunny looks just like you!" he said.

Hopper's eyes jumped from photo to photo. He couldn't believe that the bunny having so much fun in the pictures was his grandma.

10

"That's me when I learned to drive a car," Grandma said. "And that's when I played music before a big audience."

Hopper liked the pictures of Grandma playing basketball and winning a race.

"Oh, I was a fast little bunny—just like you!" said Grandma with a proud smile.

Finally, Grandma showed Hopper her favorite picture of all. It was a photograph of Grandma holding an itty-bitty baby bunny.

"That baby is you," said Grandma, hugging Hopper.

When it was time to go, Grandma gave Hopper the baby picture. She told him that next visit, they would hop down to the pond.

But Hopper shook his head. "If it's all right with you, I'd rather look through the scrapbook again."

Some Grandmas

Written by Lora Kalkman   Illustrated by Jennifer Fitchwell

Some Grandmas like golf
And some like to play cards.
Some Grandmas like taking
Good care of their yards.

Some Grandmas like dancing—
They're light on their feet!
Some Grandmas like whipping up
Sweet treats to eat.

Some Grandmas like bowling
And some like to sew.
Some like to make music
Wherever they go.

Some Grandmas can juggle
   Four big purple plums.
Some wear lots of rings
   On their fingers and thumbs.

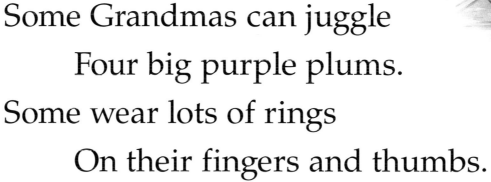

Some Grandmas like drawing
   With paints or a pen.
Some need a wee bit
   Of our help now and then.

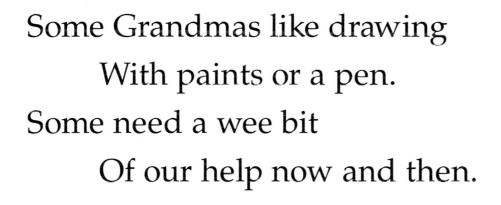

All Grandmas have something
   That sets them apart,
But they all love their grandchildren
   With all of their hearts.

A Gift for Gramma Goodie

Written by Gale Greenlee   Illustrated by Nicole Tadgell

Gramma Goodie visits her grandkids every Sunday afternoon. Every visit starts the same. First she rings the doorbell. Then Chris bounces down the stairs. Jamie runs to open the door. And every time, Gramma Goodie has gifts. But the kids never know what she'll bring.

Sometimes it's stuff you need, like socks or underwear.
Sometimes it's movie tickets or a giant teddy bear.
It could be a kite or a stuffed baby kangaroo.
It could be a lollipop that turns your tongue bright blue.

14

Well, one Sunday, Gramma rang the doorbell. Chris hurried down the stairs. And Jamie threw open the door.

"Hello, my darlings," Gramma Goodie said with a smile. "Look what I have for you." She pulled out a deck of cards, and they played "Go Fish" all afternoon.

At the end of the day, Gramma gave everyone kisses. Then she said her good-byes. As she drove away, Chris and Jamie heard their parents talking. They said that Gramma Goodie's birthday was next Sunday. They were going to plan a special dinner and bake a delicious cake for her birthday surprise.

"Gramma Goodie has a birthday?" they thought. Both were a little confused. Grown-ups have birthdays? Who in the world knew?

"Well, we have to get her a gift," Jamie decided. "But what?" asked Chris. "Gramma Goodie has absolutely EVERYTHING!"

Jamie thought about scarves, flowers, and perfume. But Gramma had plenty of scarves, a humongous rose garden, and bottles of French perfume. Chris thought about books and pillows, photo albums, and a flute.

A diary? She had one.
An umbrella? She had that, too.
A radio? There's one in her kitchen.
Oh, what would Chris and Jamie do?

They spent all week thinking. They thought in math class. They daydreamed during recess. They thought themselves to sleep! Nothing came to mind.

On Sunday, the doorbell rang. Chris didn't jump down the stairs. And Jamie didn't rush to the door.

As always, Gramma Goodie had gifts. She gave Jamie some butterscotch and Chris some peppermint. They thanked her and left to think about Gramma's gift.

All through dinner, the kids were silent as mice.

"Now I can't have you upset on my birthday," said Gramma. "What's wrong with you two?"

"Gramma, we really wanted to give you something for your birthday," Jamie said.

"But nothing we thought of would do," added Chris.

Gramma Goodie smiled and scooped the kids up in her arms. Then she whispered in their ears. "Oh, kids, don't you know? You two are the best gifts I could ever ask for."

Jumblebee

Written by Kurt Hettinger   Illustrated by Art Alvarez

Once there was a bug named Jumblebee who lived with his mother. They were very poor, and Jumblebee's mother worked hard, but Jumblebee was so lazy that he never worked at all. He slept in the shade under flowers on hot days, and dozed in front of the warm fire on cold days.

Jumblebee's mother was fed up with her son's laziness. "Tomorrow you must go find work," she told him.

The very next day, Jumblebee worked in a farmer bug's field, picking weeds. At the end of the day, the farmer gave Jumblebee a penny for his pay. But on the walk home, Jumblebee stumbled and dropped the money into a river.

"Oh, Jumblebee," said his mother, "if you had put the penny in your pocket, you wouldn't have dropped it."

"Mother, I'll be sure to do that next time," said Jumblebee. "I promise."

The very next day, Jumblebee worked for a beekeeper who gave him a cup of honey for his day's work. On the way home, Jumblebee put the cup in his pocket. But as he walked, the honey dripped and dribbled out of the cup.

When Jumblebee got home, his mother immediately saw what had happened. "You sticky, silly bug!" she said. "You could have carried that honey more steadily on your head."

"I'll be sure to do that next time," said Jumblebee. "I promise."

Bright and early the following day, Jumblebee went to work for the farmer bug again.

This time the farmer bug paid Jumblebee with a large pat of butter. Before his walk home, Jumblebee placed the butter carefully on his head. But at the end of the long, hot walk, the butter had melted all over Jumblebee's head!

"My buttery boy," said his mother, "you could have kept the butter out of the sun by holding it carefully in your hands."

"I'll do it that way next time," he said.

The next day, Jumblebee went to work for a baker who paid him unkindly with a jumpy grasshopper. Jumblebee carefully picked up the grasshopper and began walking home. Before he had gone very far, the grasshopper had scratched Jumblebee's tummy so much that Jumblebee had to let the grasshopper hop away.

When he got home, his mother sighed and said, "Son, you should have tied the grasshopper with a string and made it hop along behind you."

"I'll be sure to do that next time," said Jumblebee.

Jumblebee then worked a full day for a butcher, who paid him by giving him a heavy wheel of cheese.

Jumblebee tied the cheese with a string and dragged it behind him in the dirt. By the time he arrived home, the cheese looked like a wheel of mud. His mother was a bit cross with him for ruining the cheese.

"We can't eat that cheese now," she said to Jumblebee. "You should have carried it over your shoulder."

"I'll make sure to do that next time," said Jumblebee.

The next day Jumblebee worked at the Toad Rodeo. At the end of the rodeo, the toad wrangler gave him a toad as payment. Jumblebee had a hard time lifting the heavy toad over his shoulder, but he managed to do it. He began to walk home slowly with his wiggly toad.

Now, a beautiful young ladybug and her father lived on the road to Jumblebee's house. The poor ladybug couldn't speak at all. The doctors said she would never make any sound until she was first able to laugh. But the ladybug was far too sad to laugh at even the best, funniest jokes.

22

The young ladybug happened to look out her window just in time to see Jumblebee carrying his toad. The sight of Jumblebee struggling to hold his squirmy toad was so silly that the young ladybug smiled, then giggled, and finally burst out with a loud hoot of laughter. At that moment she was able to talk.

The ladybug was so happy that she asked Jumblebee to marry her, and he said yes. Jumblebee loved his ladybug wife very well and he began to work very hard. They lived in a large house, and Jumblebee's mother lived with the two young bugs happily ever after.

What Makes Me Special?

Written by Joanna Spathis   Illustrated by Jan Foletta

I hopped to the bakery
    For a carrot cake treat.
The baker said, "Do you know
    You have your grandpa's feet?

My teacher says I'm good at math,
    Just like my sister Lu.
Then she said that I have
    The same smile as Lu, too!

At the market, in line,
    As I waited to buy cheese,
A woman said she recognized
    My mother in my sneeze!

I wonder, if on any branch
Of this great family tree,
Is there a part of myself
That belongs just to me?

Grandma says that though I pitch
As fast as Auntie Flo,
My famous split-fingered slider
Is a throw Flo doesn't know.

No one Grandma remembers
Can sing a song as fine.
And no one has a giggle
That sounds as sweet as mine.
Grandma says, that while it is true
I take things from the rest,
The parts that make me special
Are the parts that she loves best!

The Velveteen Rabbit

Adapted by Cynthia Benjamin and Megan Musgrave   Illustrated by Phil Bliss and Jim Bliss

One bright Easter morning, a little boy woke up to find a wonderful basket in his playroom. Among the chocolates and toys was a soft, velveteen rabbit. The boy played with his rabbit until it was time for dinner.

Once the boy left the room, the other toys in the playroom began to talk to the rabbit.

"I can walk," said the robot. "Someday, I'll be real."

"What's real?" asked the rabbit.

"Real is when a child loves you very much for a long, long time," said Old Horse, the wisest toy in the playroom.

"Come on, Bunny," said the boy, returning to the playroom. "It's bedtime." The boy took the rabbit to bed with him and held him close all night. The rabbit felt warm and cozy.

"This must be what it feels like to be loved," thought the rabbit. "Someday I am going to be real."

One day the boy put the rabbit in his red wagon and they took a walk through the woods. When the boy left the rabbit to search for treasures, a furry creature came out from behind the trees. "What are you?" the creature asked the rabbit.

"I'm a rabbit, just like you!" said the velveteen rabbit.

"But you can't move," said the creature. "You can't be real."

"Yes, I am," said the rabbit. "The boy loves me, so I'm real."

As the years passed, the velveteen rabbit's fur wore away from being hugged so much by the boy. But the rabbit didn't mind. He was happy to be loved.

One day, the little boy became sick. The doctor told the boy's parents to take him to the seaside so he could rest. The boy didn't want the velveteen rabbit to get sick, too, so he left the rabbit under their favorite tree in the woods. "I'll be back," the boy whispered.

The rabbit became very sad. He was so sad that he began to cry. A real tear slid down his velveteen cheek.

Suddenly, as the rabbit looked down, a flower grew out of the spot where his tear had fallen. The blue petals of the flower slowly opened, and out flew a beautiful fairy.

"Don't cry," said the fairy. "I am the fairy of playroom magic. When toys have been loved by a child as much as the boy loved you, I make them real!"

With that, the fairy gently kissed the velveteen rabbit. "I can move!" cried the rabbit as he started to hop around.

The rabbit joined a group of other rabbits. They ran through the woods, hopping and playing.

Months later, the boy returned. Suddenly, a rabbit hopped up to him. "You're my velveteen rabbit, aren't you?" the boy asked as the rabbit winked at him. "I always knew you were real! I will come to visit you as often as I can!"

The Swing

Written by Robert Louis Stevenson   Illustrated by Sue Williams

How do you like to go up in a swing,
  Up in the air so blue?
Oh, I do think it the pleasantest thing
  Ever a child can do!

Up in the air and over the wall,
  Till I can see so wide,
Rivers and trees and cattle and all
  Over the countryside—

Till I look down on the garden green,
  Down on the roof so brown—
Up in the air I go flying again,
  Up in the air and down!

The Land of Nod

Written by Robert Louis Stevenson   Illustrated by Sue Williams

From breakfast on through all the day
    At home among my friends I stay,
But every night I go abroad
    Afar into the land of Nod.

The strangest things are there for me,
    Both things to eat and things to see,
And many frightening sights abroad
    Till morning in the land of Nod.

Try as I like to find the way,
    I never can get back by day,
Nor can remember plain and clear
    The curious music that I hear.

The Prettiest Picture

Written by Karima Amin   Illustrated by Felicia Marshall

Miss Mary Mack, Mack, Mack,
All dressed in black, black, black.

Ayanna and Grandma slapped, clapped, and sang together in the backyard. "Ooooo, Grandma! That was fun! What are we gonna do next?" asked Ayanna.

Splish! Splash! Splish! Splash!

"Uh-oh, Ayanna. Looks like rain. Let's go inside." Ayanna and Grandma picked up toys in the yard … quick! quick! … then went into the house … quick! quick!

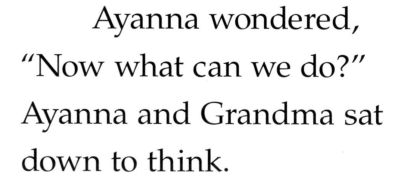

Ayanna wondered, "Now what can we do?" Ayanna and Grandma sat down to think.

"Watch television?" "Gives me the blues."

"Read a story?" "Can't seem to choose."

"Build a tower?" "Where are the blocks?"

"Play 'Old Maid'?" "Oops…no cards in the box!"

"Bake some cookies?" "It's too hot."

"Paint a picture?" "Sure…why not!"

"Well now, what can we paint?" Ayanna asked.

And Grandma answered, "I know —
let's paint the prettiest thing we can think of."

Ayanna thought to herself, "What am I
going to paint?" Ayanna thought…and then
thought some more. So many pretty,
pretty things: the big apple tree in
Grandma's backyard, the shining
sun, her favorite rag doll, a colorful
rainbow, Grandma's little cat,
hearts, flowers, smiles.

Then Ayanna had a great
big, colorful idea!

"I'll paint *all* the different pretty things I can think of," said Ayanna.

She used *all* the colors of the rainbow: red and orange, green and blue, shiny yellow, purple, too.

And she used *all* the brushes: long and short, fat and skinny, stiff and soft.

"Oh, Grandma! This is fun, fun, fun! Come here and see, Grandma! See what I've done!"

Grandma's big smile made Ayanna feel so proud.

"What did you paint, Grandma? A bird? A tree? Your cat? A rainbow? A cake? A smile?"

"There," Grandma said, "I'm done! This is definitely the prettiest thing I can think of."

"Show me, please!" Ayanna said.

Grandma showed her work.

Ayanna's eyes were big with surprise. "Grandma! Grandma, that's me!"

"That's right, sweetheart. You are the prettiest thing I could think of. Your face, smooth and brown like chocolate...your eyes like two bright stars...your hair, all twisty and curly just like Mommy's...and your beautiful smile—make you the prettiest thing I ever did see!"

My Shadow

Written by *Robert Louis Stevenson*   Illustrated by *Kallen Godsey*

I have a little shadow that goes in and out with me,
　　And what can be the use of him is more than I can see.
He is very, very like me from the heels up to the head;
　　And I see him jump before me when I jump into my bed.

The funniest thing about him is the way he likes to grow—
　　Not at all like proper children, which is always very slow;
For he sometimes shoots up taller like an india-rubber ball,
　　And he sometimes goes so little that there's none of him at all.

He hasn't got a notion of how children ought to play,

And can only make a fool of me in every sort of way.

He stays so close behind me, he's a coward you can see;

I'd think shame to stick to nursie as that shadow sticks to me!

One morning, very early, before the sun was up,

I rose and found the shining dew on every buttercup;

But my lazy little shadow, like an arrant sleepy-head,

Had stayed at home behind me and was fast asleep in bed.

The Penguin Family Picnic

Written by Kate Hannigan   Illustrated by Pat Murry Lucas

Peter Penguin had an idea. The family picnic happened only once a year, so why not take a family photo?

"How will I gather everyone?" Peter wondered.

Peter ran over to get his uncles, who were busy making popsicles. Uncle Patrick said they needed a helper.

"I can't help out now," Peter said. "I'm trying to organize a family photo, can't you see?"

"Good luck," his uncle said without moving.

Peter waddled over to tell his aunts, who were having a slipping and sliding contest. The aunts were laughing too hard to even hear Peter.

Then Peter saw his cousins ducking behind an igloo. "It's time for the family photo," Peter called.

The cousins giggled and whispered, "We can't now, Peter. We're playing hide and seek."

Peter was sad. No one was ready for the big family photograph. Everyone was too interested in having fun.

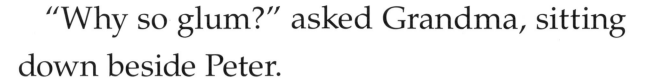

"Why so glum?" asked Grandma, sitting down beside Peter.

Peter told her how he wanted to take the picture, but everyone was too busy.

Grandma smiled. She told Peter that having a picture of the whole family together was a wonderful idea. She said it was an important idea, too, because it would remind everyone of the great fun they had at their family picnic.

"But being part of the fun moments is just as important as preserving them, don't you think?" Grandma asked.

Peter nodded. He knew his Grandma was right.

"So," Grandma said, "are you ready to have some fun now?"

"Sure!" said Peter.

With a twinkle in her eye, Grandma started a snowball fight. After a while, everyone joined in. Snowballs were flying, and penguins were laughing!

Peter Penguin laughed the hardest. He spent the rest of the afternoon sliding, skating, sledding, and smiling!

Peter Penguin had a wonderful time at the Penguin family picnic. He even managed to get a few great photographs of the fun.

"Say 'frosty,'" Peter shouted.

"Frosty!" everyone cheered.

Over in the Meadow

Written by Olive A. Wadsworth   Illustrated by Cathy Johnson

Over in the meadow in the sand in the sun,
Lived an old mother turtle and her little turtle one.
"Dig," said the mother; "I dig," said the one,
     And they dug all day in the sand in the sun.

Over in the meadow where the stream runs blue,
     Lived an old mother fish and her little fishies two.
"Swim," said the mother; "We swim," said the two,
     And they swam all day where the stream runs blue.

Over in the meadow in a hole in the tree,
    Lived an old mother owl and her little owls three.
"Whoo," said the mother; "We whoo," said the three,
    And they whooed all day in the hole in the tree.

Over in the meadow by the old barn door,
    Lived an old mother rat and her little ratties four.
"Gnaw," said the mother; "We gnaw," said the four,
    And they gnawed all day on by the old barn door.

Over in the meadow in a snug beehive,
    Lived an old mother bee and her little bees five.
"Buzz," said the mother; "We buzz," said the five,
    And they buzzed all day in the snug beehive.

Over in the meadow in a nest built of sticks,
　　Lived an old mother crow and her little crows six.
"Caw," said the mother; "We caw," said the six,
　　And they cawed all day in the nest built of sticks.

Over in the meadow where the grass grows so even,
　　Lived an old mother frog and her little froggies seven.
"Jump," said the mother; "We jump," said the seven,
　　And they jumped all day where the grass grows so even.

Over in the meadow by the old mossy gate,
  Lived an old mother lizard and her little lizards eight.
"Bask," said the mother; "We bask," said the eight,
  And they basked all day by the old mossy gate.

Over in the meadow by the old scotch pine,
  Lived an old mother duck and her little duckies nine.
"Quack," said the mother; "We quack," said the nine,
  And they quacked all day by the old scotch pine.

Over in the meadow in a cozy, wee den,
  Lived an old mother beaver and her little beavers ten.
"Beave," said the mother, "We beave," said the ten,
  And they beaved all day in their cozy, wee den.

Camp Grandma

Written by Kate Hannigan   Illustrated by Benton Mahan

Suzy Bear sat on her bed and heaved a heavy sigh. It was time to pack for Grandma's house. What should she bring?

"I can't go without Teddy," Suzy said. She tucked her stuffed bear into the suitcase. Then she added her other animals. She might need them to play with, she thought.

Suzy was afraid she might get bored. "I'll need my books," she said, "and my beach ball, my baseball mitt, my building blocks, my piggy bank, and maybe even my accordion."

Mama Bear came in to help. "What will I do there?" Suzy asked her. Mama Bear told Suzy about all the things she did growing up on the farm.

"Teddy and the other toys will be fun to play with," Mama said. "But let's pack your swimsuit—just in case you want to try something new."

"I don't think I'll like swimming in a pond," Suzy said.

Suzy felt butterflies flutter in her tummy. She had never spent the night away from home. She hugged her teddy bear as they drove to Grandma's farm.

When they arrived, Suzy could see her aunts and uncles and cousins waving.

"Suzy's here!" they cheered. When Suzy climbed out of the car, Grandma swept her up in a big bear hug.

"Your cousins have been waiting for you!" Grandma said. "They would like you to go swimming with them. Did you bring your swimsuit?"

Suzy smiled and nodded. "You bet!"

The Turnip

Adapted by Kerri Kennedy   Illustrated by Hector Borlasca

A farmer once planted some turnip seeds. "Grow, seeds, grow," he said. And they did. But one turnip grew faster than the rest. It was enormous!

One day the farmer wanted turnip stew. He grabbed the huge turnip and pulled. But the turnip just would not turn up.

So the farmer asked his wife for help. They pulled and pulled, but that turnip just would not turn up.

The wife fetched the boy and girl next door. The boy pulled the girl, who pulled the wife, who pulled the farmer, who pulled the turnip. But that turnip just would not turn up.

The girl and the boy called for their cat and dog. The cat pulled the dog, who pulled the boy, who pulled the girl, who pulled the wife, who pulled the farmer, who pulled the turnip. But that turnip just would not turn up.

The cat meowed for the mouse. The mouse pulled the cat, who pulled the dog, who pulled the boy, who pulled the girl, who pulled the wife, who pulled the farmer, who pulled the turnip. But that turnip just would not turn up!

Along came a ladybug. She reached out and gave the wife's skirt a tiny tug. And do you know what happened? The earth cracked, and pop! The turnip turned up.

That night, the farmer, the wife, the boy, the girl, the dog, the cat, the mouse, and the ladybug dined on the tastiest turnip stew ever imagined.

Grandma's Garden

Written by Karima Amin   Illustrated by Cathy Johnson

Today's the day!
We're going to see Grandma and Grandpa.

I've got my suitcase and my teddy, and I'm ready.

My grandma is love—

Pillow-soft lap, biscuit-warm hugs,

And honey-sweet kisses all over my face!

My grandpa makes me laugh.

He's a tickle and a joke, and a pocketful of peppermint.

Grandpa's hugs are big-man strong.

His kiss is quick, like a high five.

My grandma has a garden.
Flowers, big and small, and plenty good things to eat.
The garden is a magic place
Where wiggly worms, as long as my arms,
Squiggle in the sweet-smelling dirt,
And ladybugs tell me their secrets.

There are fat red tomatoes as big as watermelons,
And watermelons as big as baby elephants!
Once when I bit into a watermelon,
The juice gooshed down my chin so much,
I was swimming in a pool of pink juice!

When we dug up sweet pataters,
We had to dig and pull and pull and dig.
The roots went all the way to Africa!
With my ear near the ground,
I heard people singing!
An African child called my name!

So many colors! Reds! Greens! Yellows!

Already I can taste cool cucumbers, sweet tomatoes,

And yummy watermelons.

I can already feel my Grandma's warm hug!

I'm getting a little tired now. "Are we there yet?" I ask.

Mommy says, "Not yet." Daddy says, "Soon."

We ride and ride … until Daddy shouts, "Here we are!"

Grandma, wearing her sun hat, comes out to see us.
"Hello! Hello! How's my special sweet patater?"
Her hug is as warm and soft as I remembered.
She makes me smile from my nose to my toes.

"Grandma, may I see the garden?"
"Sure, Baby. Let's go!" she says.

"Look at those watermelons!"
They don't look so big but Grandma says,
"They're ready for eating."
Mmmmmm … watermelon for lunch. Juicy! Juicy! Juicy!

A ladybug stops to rest on my arm.
She whispers, "Welcome back.
I missed you."

What Instrument Should I Play?

Written by Lora Kalkman   Illustrated by Dara Goldman

Junior asked his mom what instrument he should play.

"I like music that swings," she replied. "Jazz suits me." Junior's mom explained that jazz musicians play curvy brass saxophones that *trill, trill!* They play piano keys that *clink, clink, clink!*

"What do you think, Dad?" asked Junior.

Junior's dad said, "I like music that sings. Classical music suits me." He explained that classical musicians play violins that *hum, hum!* They play shiny silver flutes that *chirp, chirp, chirp!*

"This is a hard decision," Junior said. "What do you think, Grandma?" he asked.

"I love all kinds of music. And all instruments sound beautiful when they are played well," Grandma said with a wink. "If you pick the instrument YOU love most and practice hard, you can't go wrong."

The next day Junior and his family visited the music store. Junior tried instruments that chirped and hummed, clinked and trilled. Then Junior remembered his Grandma's advice.

"This is the one I like most!" Junior said with a *boom, boom!*

Grandma smiled. "A wonderful choice. The drums are a personal favorite of mine, too!"

The Day Rabbit Came for Pie

Adapted by T.J. Dugan   Illustrated by Jane Maday

Lisa loved pie. She loved lemon and blueberry, peach and rhubarb, but her favorite was her Grandma Abigail's not-too-sweet, not-too-tart apple pie.

One rainy afternoon, Lisa asked her mother if she could go to Grandma's house for pie. "Grandma can't pick apples in the rain," her mother said.

"I can pick the apples," Lisa said. So she gathered her warmest raincoat, her floppiest hat, her favorite umbrella, and her galoshes. Truthfully, her galoshes were a little too big, but she'd grow into them.

Lisa set off to pick apples. Soon she realized that no matter how she stretched, she couldn't reach any apples!

A bear stopped to help.
"If I pick apples for you, will
you give me your hat?" he
asked. "I can't see in this rain."
Lisa agreed. But the bear
tricked her. As soon as he had her hat, he
said, "I see now that I will not help you. Good-bye."
"If I had an umbrella," said a passing fox, "I'd take
a nap under it. I'll help you in exchange for your umbrella."
Lisa agreed. But once Lisa handed him the umbrella,
he yawned and said, "Good night, it's time for my nap."
A wolf walked up. "I'll help, but it would be quite
gracious of you to give me your coat in exchange.
My fur has been damp all spring." But the
wolf tricked her, too.
"I'd love to help, but my feet slip,"
said a passing rabbit. "Nice boots!"
"Take them," Lisa sighed.
"They're too big for me anyway."

"Why the long face?" the rabbit asked Lisa. "With your galoshes, I can jump to incredible heights." The rabbit jumped and picked three apples. "You may not have your clothes, but you'll have pie!" shouted the rabbit.

The rabbit's jumping and shouting made the animals come running. "I was sleeping," the wolf growled. "But did I hear you say pie?"

The bear saw the fox's umbrella. "My hat is a little small," he said. "Give me that umbrella. What pie?"

"Where are your manners?" said the wolf. "*I'd* like the umbrella, *please,* and a warm piece of pie as well."

The animals began to argue and chase one another around the apple tree.

58

The bear chased the fox. The fox chased the wolf. The wolf chased the bear, shouting that chasing wasn't good manners! The animals ran around and around the apple tree, shedding the hat, coat, and umbrella as they went.

All their running caused the ground to shake…which caused the apples to drop!

"Hurry," said the rabbit. "With your galoshes, I can run at incredible speeds! Grab your things, and fill your basket. You'll be eating pie soon!"

The two new friends fled to Grandma Abigail's house, where she took the apples and made delicious pies for them to share. And that's what happened the day rabbit came for pie.

The Little Land

Written by Robert Louis Stevenson   Illustrated by Rob Hefferan

When at home alone I sit
    And am very tired of it,
I have to just shut my eyes
    To go sailing through the skies—
To go sailing far away
    To the pleasant Land of Play;
To the fairy land afar
    Where the little people are;
Where the clover-tops are trees,
    And the rain-pools are the seas,
And the leaves like little ships
    Sail about on tiny trips;
And above the daisy tree
    Through the grasses,
High o'erhead the bumble bee
    Hums and passes.

Grandma's Hot Chocolate

Written by Joanna Spathis   Illustrated by Margie Moore

Her kitchen is toasty
And she has set out two mugs
filled with creamy, warm chocolate,
   As warm as her hugs!

It is rarely too hot
   And never too cold.
But what makes it best—
   Or so I am told—

Is that, besides the chocolate
   And the marshmallow or two,
She makes it with love
   And especially for you!

Pearl Learns to Knit

Written by Rebecca Grazulis   Illustrated by Susan Banta

Snug in her den, there is a frustrated bear cub who cannot knit yet. Her name is Pearl, and she is six. Pearl can do lots of things well. She can set the dinner table. She can pick berries. And she can hibernate like a pro.

Knitting, however, is another story. Her Grandma Kelly is trying to teach her, but the lessons are not going well.

"I want to make a hat," Pearl told her Grandma Kelly.

"Patience, little one," said Grandma Kelly. "It takes time to learn something new."

"Grandma," Pearl asked, "did you make mistakes when you were learning to knit?"

"Of course," Grandma Kelly said. "I made lots of mistakes! And I still make mistakes now. Knitting takes lots of practice. Don't worry about mistakes."

Pearl smiled. It was a lot easier to practice knitting when she didn't worry about mistakes.

Pearl lifted up the socks she was working on and sighed. They were too big— even for her Papa Bear.

Grandma Kelly put on the socks. "These are the coziest socks ever made!" she said.

Pearl shyly held out the scarf she was working on.

Grandma Kelly tried on the huge scarf. "I love it!" she said. "This scarf will keep us ALL warm this winter!"

Pearl learned to knit. And maybe if she practices and practices, she will even get better and better!

Cooking Up a Storm

Written by Vincent F. A. Golphin   Illustrated by Ron Husband

B*a ... room!* The sound rolled on the night air like giants' footsteps. *Ba ... room!*

Elijah Jeremiah closed his eyes and snuggled under the bedcovers as the *ba ... room* sound of the storm grew every minute, coming faster, and louder, and closer to his room.

In his mind, the storm was a man as tall as the tallest mountain, whose long watery arms splashed rain. The thunder and lightning were the man's angry, stomping feet.

The boy hid his eyes, but no matter how hard he tried, he couldn't close his ears.

"*Craaaack … Pitt-ow!*" went the lightning. The room shook.

Elijah Jeremiah tried to be brave, but he could not look out the window. He had once heard his Aunt Mae say that storms happen when giants come out to play. The thunder boomed. It sure sounded like giants. Elijah shuddered under the covers.

Elijah Jeremiah finally peeked above the covers. He looked out the window and saw the elm tree dance around the backyard.

The not-so-brave little boy shivered in the darkness and counted raindrops against the windows. One … ten … thirty; they fell fast. The raindrops sounded like little fingers tapping against the window. As the lightning's brightness bounced off the walls, the sound of the rain put Elijah Jeremiah to sleep.

In the morning, Elijah Jeremiah heard his dad down in the kitchen. "I can't wait," his father said. "My mother is gonna cook up a storm tonight."

"Oh, no," Elijah Jeremiah thought. "Grandma cooks up storms! How awful!" He imagined the winds and rain of the night before.

Elijah Jeremiah climbed into the back seat of the car for the drive to Grandma's house. He sat quietly, like a tiny mouse.

They arrived at Grandma's house. Elijah Jeremiah walked slowly inside, expecting to hear thunder's rumble any moment. Instead, he only heard the cheerful clatter of pots and pans. And instead of lightning, he saw a big, juicy ham and a pot of greens! The delicious smells lifted his gloom.

Grandma brought a pecan pie to the table. "Hope you're hungry, E.J.," she said. "I've cooked up a storm!"

The family ate and ate until their bellies felt tight. Elijah Jeremiah patted his tummy. "Grandma, this was the yummiest storm I ever ate!" he said. He was never afraid of storms again.

Snow Days

Written by Amy Adair Illustrated by Michelle Berg

Billy thought snow days were boring. There was never anything fun to do. "Come outside with me," Grandpa called. "On snow days when I was a boy, I played with this toboggan."

Billy followed Grandpa up a hill. "One, two, three!" they counted together. Then they jumped onto the toboggan.

Whoosh! They sailed down the hill again and again.

"Brrr," Billy shivered. "It's getting cold out here."

"Let's go in and warm up," Grandpa said.

Inside the cozy house, Grandma was waiting with hot chocolate and cookies.

"Grandpa," Billy said, "tell me more about when you were a boy."

Grandpa smiled. "My favorite days were snow days, because my grandpa—your great-great grandpa—took me sledding in that very same toboggan."

"Snow days are my favorite days, too!" Billy said. "I can't wait until the next one."

"Neither can I," Grandpa said with a huge smile.

A Story for Squeakins

Written by Brooke Zimmerman   Illustrated by Teri Weidner

One day, it was time for Squeakins Mouse to take a nap. "All right now, dearest deary dear, it is time to take your nap." This was said by none other than dear old, gray old Granny Mouse.

"Oh, but my dear Granny dear, I couldn't possibly take a nap … not without first hearing a story!" replied none other than cute little, sweet little Squeakins Mouse.

"All right then, dearest deary dear," said dear gray Granny. "And what kind of story would you like?"

"A nice one, I think," said cute sweet Squeakins. "One with a nice happy ending."

So Granny went to fetch the happiest-ending storybook she could find. But on her way to the bookshelf, she ran into a bit of trouble. She ran into big old, mean old Mittens the cat.

"Oh, Ratty!" said Mittens Catty. "What a nice treat you'd be to eat."

"Oh, no!" said dear gray Granny to big mean Mittens. "You must let me pass, for I must fetch a nice happy storybook to read to cute sweet Squeakins!"

"I see," said big mean Mittens with a growl and a yowl. "I'll let you pass if you bring me some milk from the cow."

So Granny scurried straight to mooey old, brown old Bessie to ask for some milk. "Mooey brown Bessie, may I have some fresh cold milk to give to big mean Mittens so I can pass?" asked dear gray Granny. "I must fetch a nice happy storybook for cute sweet little Squeakins!"

And mooey brown Bessie said, "Very well. I'll give you some milk if you bring me a new brass cowbell."

So Granny scurried straight to grizzly old, twizzly old Tom Tinker to ask for a brass cowbell.

"Grizzly twizzly Tinker, may I have a clangy bangy brass cowbell to give to mooey brown Bessie so she will give me fresh milk to give to big mean Mittens so I can pass?" asked dear gray Granny. "I must fetch a nice happy storybook for cute sweet Squeakins!"

"Yes, I will give you a cowbell of brass," said grizzly twizzly Tinker, "if you'll bring me some lemonade in a glass!" (For it was a very hot day.)

So Granny scurried straight to the leafy old, tall old lemon tree to ask for some lemons.

"Leafy tall tree, may I have some round yellow lemons to make tart lickety lemonade to give to grizzly twizzly Tinker so he will give me a clangy bangy brass cowbell to give to mooey brown Bessie so she will give me fresh cold milk to give to big mean Mittens so I can pass?" asked dear gray Granny. "I must fetch a nice happy storybook for cute sweet Squeakins!"

"I'll give
you a lemon, or
two, or three," said
leafy tall tree, "if you'll
get some water to sprinkle
on me!" (For it was a very
hot day.)

So Granny scurried
straight to the middle of the
yard. There she stood and
looked straight, straight up to
ask the puffy old, fluffy old
clouds for some water.

"Puffy fluffy clouds, may I have some cool wet water to sprinkle on leafy tall tree so he will give me a round yellow lemon to make tart lickety lemonade to give to grizzly twizzly Tinker?" Granny took a breath. "So Tinker will give me a clangy bangy brass cowbell to give to mooey brown Bessie so she will give me fresh cold milk to give to big mean Mittens so I can pass?" asked dear gray Granny. "I must fetch a nice happy storybook for cute sweet Squeakins!" And the fluffy puffy clouds said, "*BOOM!*" and it began to rain.

Well! What do you think happened next?

The clouds gave water.

The tree gave a lemon.

Tom Tinker gave a cowbell.

Bessie gave some milk.

Mittens let Granny pass.

And Granny fetched a storybook to read to cute sweet Squeakins. But by the time Granny got back ... Squeakins was already asleep!

Grandma's Attic

Written by Lora Kalkman   Illustrated by Benton Mahan

Here's the hat that I wore when I dined with the king.
Grandpa gave me this necklace and big purple ring.
This shawl was a gift from MY grandma, you see —
She knit it for me when I had a baby.

I danced in these shoes when I went to the ball.
I wore these white gloves to the ballet one fall.
In this dress, I sipped tea on a train bound for Cork.
And I carried this purse when I shopped in New York.
All these things were quite special to me in the day,
Now I love watching you dress up in them to play!

Bed in Summer

Written by Robert Louis Stevenson   Illustrated by Angela Jarecki

In winter I get up at night
　　And dress by yellow candlelight.
In summer quite the other way,
　　I have to go to bed by day.

　I have to go to bed and see
　　　The birds still hopping on the tree,
Or hear the grown-up people's feet
　　　Still going past me in the street.

And does it not seem hard to you,
　　When all the sky is clear and blue,
And I should like so much to play,
　　To have to go to bed by day?

Grandma's Fishing Trip

Written by Kate Hannigan   Illustrated by Janice Kinnealy

Grandma went fishing every Saturday morning. But today was a very special Saturday because Grandma was bringing some very special frogs with her. "Wake up, my little ones," said Grandma. "It is time to catch some fish! What a special day."

Hoppy and Leapy sprung out of bed. They had never gone fishing with their grandma, and they were very excited. They threw off their pajamas and brushed their long tongues.

Grandma helped the little frogs pack their fly and beetlebug jam sandwiches. They gathered their gear, and they were on their way.

It truly was a beautiful day. The pond water was still, the sun was shining, and the sky was clear. The three frogs pulled out their gear and cast their fishing lines. They talked and talked and talked and fished all day long. When they were hungry, they ate their fly and beetlebug jam sandwiches.

Soon the sun began to set over the hills, and the sky turned a soft pink. It was time to go. "Let's go tell Grandpa about my best fishing day ever!" Grandma said, smiling.

"But we didn't catch any fish!" croaked the kids. "How can it be your best day ever?"

Grandma pulled Hoppy and Leapy into her arms. "We didn't catch any fish, it's true," she said. "But it was my favorite day ever because I was able to spend it with you!"

8 1

Bicycles

Written by Joanna Spathis   Illustrated by Julie Durrell

Grandpa had a unicycle
That was the color red.
He'd roll around on just one wheel
Until he went to bed.

When he met my grandmother
One wheel no longer would do,
So he went out and found a bike
Built especially for two.

They've had many adventures,
And today they still love to ride.
Now that it's time for me to learn,
I'm lucky they're by my side.

What Do You Call Her?

Written by Gale Greenlee   Illustrated by Angela Jarecki

What do you call your grandma?
Is she Meemaw or Mamoo?
Do you call her Gram or Granny?
Mim or Pitty Poo?

Jaylin calls his gram Miss Shuga
'Cuz she smells so sweet.
To Betty, she's Creek Momma
'Cuz she lives behind the creek.

Maria calls her gram Abuela,
Or sometimes just Abu.
Boris calls his gram Babuska
And Kim likes Ludie Loo.

In China she is Nai Nai,
    In Swahili she's Sho Sho.
Some folks say Nyanya,
    And in Creole she's Go Go.

But it really doesn't matter
    What name you know her by.
You can call her Queenie, Babs, or Tati,
    Or even Miss Moon Pie!

She could be your Ya Ya,
    Your Nonnie or Nanoo,
Whatever name you call her —
    She's full of love for you.

Proud Big Brother

Written by Dennis Fertig   Illustrated by Jennifer Fitchwell

When baby Olivia cried, Daniel wanted to help. He was her big brother! But Mom and Dad would run to help her. They didn't even notice Daniel.

It was worse when she wasn't crying. If Olivia smiled or even burped, Mom and Dad would say, "Isn't she cute?" Daniel would think, "Hey, what about me?" Daniel had not expected it to be this way. He thought they would play together. Daniel thought his Mom and Dad would be proud of him because he loved his baby sister. Instead, they forgot he was around!

Sometimes Daniel just sat and felt sad. Being a big brother was not fun at all. In fact, it was downright lonely.

That's what Daniel was thinking when the doorbell rang. At first he was excited because it was Grandma! Then he thought, "She's just coming to see Olivia. Great."

But Grandma surprised Daniel. She didn't go see Olivia. Instead she said, "Hi, Daniel! I've been looking forward to seeing you all day!"

"You have?" Daniel asked.

"I sure have," Grandma said with a smile. "Let's ride our bikes to the park."

At the park, Grandma and Daniel had bike races and played on the swings. They spent the next day building a fantastic castle at the beach.

"That little sister of yours is very lucky," Grandma said. "Someday, you'll show her how to do many fun things."

Daniel said, "I don't think so, Grandma."

"Sure you will!" said Grandma. "You'll teach her how to ride a bike, how to swing, and how to build a sandcastle that a princess would love!"

"Well, Olivia is a princess," said Daniel frowning. "At least Mom and Dad treat her like a princess."

"Oh, really," said Grandma. "And how do they treat Olivia's big brother?"

"Like I'm not around," Daniel said with a sigh.

Grandma nodded. "I remember at this park last summer, I asked you to be careful on the swings. You said, 'Grandma, please don't treat me like a baby.'"

Daniel remembered that, too.

"Mom and Dad treat Olivia in a special way," said Grandma. "They treat her like a baby. They treat you in a special way, too—like a big brother who doesn't need as much of their help now, and who will help take care of Olivia."

"Someday," Grandma continued, "Olivia will treat you in a special way, too—like her big brother. Her hero."

"She will?" asked Daniel.

Grandma nodded yes.

"Can we go home now?" Daniel asked. "I have to tell Olivia about the things I'll teach her."

And that's exactly what Daniel—a proud big brother—did!

A Great Day for Sledding

Written by Leslie Lindecker   Illustrated by Rob Hefferan

Petie danced around the igloo. "New snow! New snow! We have new snow today," he sang. Petie Penguin was so excited he could not sit still long enough to eat his breakfast.

His brother Percy was excited, too. All little penguins love new snow.

"Hurry, Percy! Let's go play!" Petie cried.

Percy finished his breakfast and wrapped his scarf tight around his neck. Then Percy helped his brother put his winter hat snugly on his head.

90

"Are you ready, Petie?" asked Percy.

Petie nodded. "I sure am, Percy!"

"Then let's go!" said Percy. "This is a great day for sledding down the big hill!"

Petie and Percy Penguin began the long climb up the big hill, pulling their sled behind them. Up and up they went, much higher than Petie had ever been before.

Petie began to worry. "Uh, maybe we should stop and build snow penguins," he suggested.

Percy smiled. "But it's such a great day for sledding, Petie!"

"Well…how about making snow angels instead?" Petie said, flopping himself down in the snow.

"Aw, come on, Petie! It's a great day for sledding!" Percy said.

Percy and Petie kept climbing up. "This sure is a big hill," Petie said with a gulp. A moment later Petie said, "Maybe it's too cold up here for sledding."

Percy put his flipper around Petie's shoulders. "Don't be scared," Percy said. "We will ride down together."

Percy and Petie Penguin got to the top of the big hill. Petie got on the sled and squeezed his eyes shut. Percy got on and pushed off. Percy and Petie went flying down the big hill. Petie's eyes popped open. It was wonderful! So fast. So cold. So white!

"It's a great day for sledding," Petie said with a laugh when they got to the bottom of the hill.

"You know what?" Percy replied. "It's a great day for having a brother, too!"

The Sugarplum Tree

Written by Eugene Field   Illustrated by Kelly Grupcynski

Have you ever heard of the Sugarplum Tree?
'Tis a marvel of great renown!
It blooms on the shore of the Lollipop Sea
    In the garden of Shut-Eye Town;

When you've got to the tree, you would have a hard time
    To capture the fruit which I sing;
The tree is so tall that no person could climb
    To the boughs where the sugarplums swing!

But up in that tree sits a chocolate cat,
    And a gingerbread dog prowls below—
And this is the way you contrive to get at
    Those sugarplums tempting you so:

You say but the word to that gingerbread dog
        And he barks with such a terrible zest
That the chocolate cat is at once all agog,
        As her swelling proportions attest.

And the chocolate cat goes cavorting around
        From this leafy limb unto that,
And the sugarplums tumble, of course, to the ground—
        Hurray for that chocolate cat!

So come, little child, cuddle closer to me
        In your dainty white nightcap and gown,
And I'll rock you away to the Sugarplum Tree
        In the garden of Shut-Eye Town.

The Moon

Written by Robert Louis Stevenson Illustrated by Sue Williams

The moon has a face like the clock in the hall;
She shines on the thieves on the garden wall,
On streets and fields and harbor quays,
And birdies asleep in the fork of the trees.

The squalling cat and the squeaking mouse,
The howling dog by the door of the house.
The bat that lies in bed at noon,
All love to be out by the light of the moon.

But all of the things that belong to the day
Cuddle to sleep to be out of her way;
And flowers and children close their eyes
Till up in the morning the sun shall rise.